The Cam Jansen Series

Cam Jansen and the Mystery of the Stolen Diamonds
Cam Jansen and the Mystery of the U.F.O.
Cam Jansen and the Mystery of the Dinosaur Bones
Cam Jansen and the Mystery of the Television Dog
Cam Jansen and the Mystery of the Gold Coins
Cam Jansen and the Mystery of the Babe Ruth Baseball
Cam Jansen and the Mystery of the Circus Clown
Cam Jansen and the Mystery of the Monster Movie
Cam Jansen and the Mystery of the Carnival Prize
Cam Jansen and the Mystery at the Monkey House
Cam Jansen and the Mystery of the Stolen Corn Popper
Cam Jansen and the Mystery of Flight 54
Cam Jansen and the Mystery at the Haunted House
Cam Jansen and the Chocolate Fudge Mystery
Cam Jansen and the Triceratops Pops Mystery
Cam Jansen and the Ghostly Mystery
Cam Jansen and the Scary Snake Mystery
Cam Jansen and the Catnapping Mystery
Cam Jansen and the Barking Treasure Mystery
Cam Jansen and the Birthday Mystery
Cam Jansen and the School Play Mystery
Cam Jansen and the First Day of School Mystery
Cam Jansen and the Tennis Trophy Mystery
Cam Jansen and the Snowy Day Mystery
Cam Jansen and the Valentine Baby Mystery—25th Anniversary Special
Cam Jansen and the Secret Service Mystery
Cam Jansen and the Summer Camp Mysteries—A Super Special
Cam Jansen and the Mystery Writer Mystery
Cam Jansen and the Green School Mystery

DON'T FORGET ABOUT THE YOUNG CAM JANSEN
SERIES FOR YOUNGER READERS!

CamJansen

and the Sports Day Mysteries

A SUPER SPECIAL

by David A. Adler

illustrated by
Joy Allen

VIKING

VIKING
Published by Penguin Group
Penguin Young Readers Group, 345 Hudson Street, New York, New York 10014, U.S.A.
Penguin Group (Canada), 90 Eglinton Avenue East, Suite 700, Toronto,
Ontario, Canada M4P 2Y3 (a division of Pearson Penguin Canada Inc.)
Penguin Books Ltd, 80 Strand, London WC2R 0RL, England
Penguin Ireland, 25 St Stephen's Green, Dublin 2,
Ireland (a division of Penguin Books Ltd)
Penguin Group (Australia), 250 Camberwell Road, Camberwell,
Victoria 3124, Australia (a division of Pearson Australia Group Pty Ltd)
Penguin Books India Pvt Ltd, 11 Community Centre,
Panchsheel Park, New Delhi – 110 017, India
Penguin Group (NZ), 67 Apollo Drive, Rosedale, North Shore 0632,
New Zealand (a division of Pearson New Zealand Ltd.)
Penguin Books (South Africa) (Pty) Ltd, 24 Sturdee Avenue,
Rosebank, Johannesburg 2196, South Africa

Penguin Books Ltd, Registered Offices: 80 Strand, London WC2R 0RL, England

Published simultaneously in the United States of America by Viking and
Puffin Books, divisions of Penguin Young Readers Group, 2009

1 3 5 7 9 10 8 6 4 2

Text copyright © David A. Adler, 2009
Illustrations copyright © Penguin Young Readers Group, 2009
Illustrations by Joy Allen
All rights reserved

LIBRARY OF CONGRESS CATALOGING-IN-PUBLICATION DATA
Adler, David A.
Cam Jansen and the Sports Day mysteries : a super special /
by David A. Adler ; illustrated by Joy Allen.
p. cm.
Summary: Supersleuth Cam Jansen solves three mysteries
during her class's Sports and Good Nutrition Day.
ISBN 978-0-14-241225-1 (pbk.)—ISBN 978-0-670-01163-6 (hardcover)
[1. Schools—Fiction. 2. Sports—Fiction. 3. Mystery and detective stories.]
I. Allen, Joy, ill. II. Title.
PZ7.A2615Caqln 2009
[Fic]
2008029568

Manufactured in China

For Dr. Reneé M. Hamada
Happy 36th!
—D.A.

To Jeff and Isaac, my baseball boys!
—J.A.

CamJansen
and the Sports Day Mysteries

A SUPER SPECIAL

CONTENTS

CamJansen
The Backward Race
Mystery

Chapter One

"Look at my face," Danny said. "You'll really want to remember it. One day you'll say you went to school with the great Danny Pace."

Beth shook her head. "That's not what I'll say," she told him. "I'll say I went to school with corny Danny Pace."

"I'm great at sports," Danny said. "I might win an Olympic gold medal.

"Maybe you'll win a medal, but it will be for bad jokes," Beth said.

Danny pretended to swing a baseball bat. *"Bam!"* he said. "Just wait until I come to bat in the baseball game. I'll hit the ball a mile."

Danny was holding a baseball glove. He pretended it was a bat and swung it right into Cam Jansen.

"Ow!" Cam said. "Put that away."

"I'm sorry," Danny said.

He put his glove on his head.

Today was Sports and Good Nutrition Day for the fifth grade. Fifth graders would go to Franklin Park. They would run races, play soccer and baseball, and have a picnic lunch.

"Franklin Park is much bigger than our schoolyard," Cam Jansen's teacher, Ms. Benson, had told the class. "That's why we're going there instead of having Sports Day at school."

Cam Jansen and her class were walking to the park. The other fifth-grade class, Mr. Dane's class, was ahead of them.

Ms. Benson turned and held up her hands. The children stopped. "Please," she said. "Let's stay together."

"Stay together," Danny's father said as he walked toward the back of the line.

Mr. Pace and several other parents had come along to help. Mrs. Wayne had come along, too. She was the principal's secretary.

"Hey," Mr. Pace whispered when he came to Danny. "When I was in fifth grade I was really great at sports. Do you know how high I could jump? I could jump higher than a house."

"Wow," Danny said. "That's really high!"

"Sure," his father told him. He laughed. "A house can't jump."

"Listen to this," Danny told his father. "Yesterday in school I saw an egg in the hall. Do you know where it came from?"

"Did it come from the cafeteria?" Mr. Pace asked.

"No," Danny said and shook his head. "It came from a hen."

"Those jokes are terrible," Beth said. "Let's get to the park."

"We'll play baseball when we get there," Danny said. "We're playing against Mr. Dane's class."

Danny stepped back, took his hands from his pockets, and swung his pretend bat again.

"I think the races are first," Mr. Pace told his son. "Then you play soccer."

"Cam can tell us," Eric Shelton said. He was Cam's best friend. "The schedule was on the board in our room. Cam just has to look at the pictures she has in her head."

Cam has what people call a photographic memory. It's as if she has lots of photographs in her head, pictures of everything she's seen. To remember something, she just looks at the pictures.

Cam closed her eyes. She said, *"Click!"*

Click is the sound a camera makes when it takes a picture. It's also the sound Cam makes when she looks at the pictures she has in her head.

"The races are first," Cam said with her eyes still closed. "There's an egg-balancing race, a potato-sack race, and a backward race. We rest. Then we play soccer, eat lunch,

rest some more, and then play baseball."

Cam's real name is Jennifer, but when people found out about her amazing photographic memory, they called her "The Camera." Soon "The Camera" became just "Cam."

Danny said, "The races and games are all against Mr. Dane's class. We've got to beat them!"

Ms. Benson and her class walked past a bookstore, a fruit store, and a bank.

"That's Zelda's Bakery," Beth said, and pointed to a store near the end of the block. "They make a chocolate cupcake with rainbow sprinkles. It's great."

"Cupcakes have lots of sugar," Mr. Pace told Beth. "I don't think anyone should eat lots of rainbow-sprinkle cupcakes."

"My dad buys the oat bran muffins," Eric said. "He says they are good for him."

Just then two old women hurried out of Zelda's.

"They're coming this way," Danny said.

Four other people hurried out of Zelda's. They went the other way.

Eric said, "There must be trouble at Zelda's."

"Maybe the sprinkles are fighting," Danny said. "Maybe they're jumping off the cup-cakes."

"This isn't funny," Beth told him. "Those women look scared."

Chapter Two

Eric said, "Maybe there's a fire at Zelda's. Fires are scary."

Cam watched the front of Zelda's. She wondered if anyone else would leave the store.

"The two women are coming this way," Beth said. "Let's ask them what happened."

They were walking slower now. One was tall and thin. The other was short and heavy. They walked past Ms. Benson and the children at the front of the line.

The larger woman stopped by the bank. She leaned against the wall. She put her hand to her heart.

"I have to rest," she said.

The thin woman stopped, too.

"Hello," Mr. Pace said to them. "Are you okay?"

The thin woman looked at her friend. "I'm okay," she said. "Sadie, are you okay?"

"Yes, Martha," the woman named Sadie said.

"What happened at Zelda's?" Beth asked.

Cam looked away from the front of the bakery. She wanted to hear what happened at Zelda's.

"It was horrible," Martha told Beth. "'Give me your money.' That's what he said."

"That's what *who* said?" Beth asked.

"The man with the floppy red hat said that," Martha answered. "He sounded angry."

"He talked real fast. I think he was in a hurry," Sadie said. "I think maybe he was on his way to his job. Maybe he didn't want to be late."

Martha shook her head and said, "You're

wrong, Sadie. That *was* his job. He's a thief."

"What else was he wearing?" Eric asked.

"He wore that big red floppy hat, an old blue jacket, blue jeans, blue sneakers, and large sunglasses," Martha answered. "We saw his clothing, but we didn't see his face. The hat and sunglasses hid it."

"That's right," Sadie said. "He also had something green with a wire attached in his ear. I think it was an earphone."

Martha said, "I think he was listening to music."

Cam closed her eyes. She said, *"Click!"*

"I saw him," Cam said with her eyes still closed. "Just after you ran out of Zelda's, he left, too. He went the other way."

Cam opened her eyes.

"Hey," Danny said. "We're going that way. Maybe we'll see him."

Sadie stepped away from the wall. She took a deep breath and said, "I feel better now."

"If we see a man in a big floppy red hat,"

Danny's father said, "we'll call the police. I brought along a cell phone."

"He took only three dollars from me," Sadie said. "That's because I take along only as much money as I need. I was buying a loaf of bread, so I just needed three dollars."

"He took more from me," Martha said. "He took lots more money and my gold bracelet." She wiped away a tear. "My children gave me that bracelet for Mother's Day."

"We have to go to the park," Mr. Pace said.

Sadie told Martha, "You'll buy another bracelet. Your children will never know the one they gave you was stolen."

"But I'll know," Martha said.

"Let's go," Mr. Pace told Danny and the others.

"My friend Cam Jansen will catch the thief," Eric told the two women. "She's a great detective. She'll get your bracelet and money back, too."

"Let's go," Danny's father said again.

"Yes," Mrs. Wayne added. "Let's go."

Cam, Danny, and Beth followed Mr. Pace and Mrs. Wayne.

Eric waited until the others were a few steps ahead. Then he whispered to the women, "Don't worry. Cam is amazing. She'll get your things back."

Sadie took a small card from her purse. She wrote on it. "This is my telephone number. Call me when she gets our things."

Eric took the small card. Then he ran to catch up with the others.

Chapter Three

A police car sped past Cam and her friends. It stopped in front of Zelda's. Two police officers got out. They went into the bakery.

Mrs. Wayne said, "I wonder what's happening in there."

"I'm wondering, too," Danny said. "I'm going in."

"No you're not," his father told him. "You're going with us to Franklin Park."

As they walked past Zelda's, Cam, Eric, Mrs. Wayne, and Danny looked in. Two police officers were there. They were talking to a very thin woman.

"That thin woman is Zelda," Eric whispered to Cam. "She loves to bake."

"Let's go," Mr. Pace said.

Just past Zelda's was a narrow driveway. Along one side of the driveway was Zelda's. Along the other side was a tall metal fence. At the end of the driveway was a large open metal trash container.

"Hey, look at that!" Danny said. "There is something red in the trash."

Danny hurried down the driveway.

"Wait! Wait!" his father called.

Mr. Pace hurried after his son.

Cam and Eric watched Danny step onto a wooden box by the side of the trash bin. He reached into the trash and took out something red.

"Look at this!" Danny said as he ran toward Cam.

Danny had a large red hat.

"I found it in the garbage," Danny said. "It was right on top."

"You shouldn't have taken that hat," Mr. Pace said. "I don't want you mixed up in any robbery. We should give that hat to the police and then go to the park."

"Yes, let's go," Beth said. "Ms. Benson is way ahead of us. *Everyone* is way ahead of us."

"Danny, that hat is a clue," Mr. Pace told his son. "You must give it to the police."

"But I like this hat," Danny said. "Look at me."

He put on the floppy red hat. He turned so everyone could see how he looked.

"Ha!" Beth said. "I bet crooks don't wash their hair much. I bet that hat has cooties."

"Cooties!" Danny said.

He threw the hat to the ground.

"I'm giving that to the police," Mrs. Wayne said. "But first, I'm looking in the trash for more clues."

Mrs. Wayne took the hat off the ground. Then she walked along the driveway toward the trash bin.

"Come on," Cam whispered to Eric. "Let's go with her."

Mrs. Wayne, Cam, and Eric hurried down the driveway. Eric stood on the box by the side of the bin and looked in.

"Just look," Mrs. Wayne told him. "Don't touch anything."

Eric said, "I see a large pair of sunglasses."

Cam told Eric to look for a blue jacket.

"There it is," Eric said. "And there's a green wire hanging out of the pocket. I bet that's the wire Sadie and Martha saw."

Cam and Eric looked around the trash

bin. The area was clean. The driveway and backyard of the bakery were surrounded by the metal fence.

Eric said, "We knew the thief was wearing a large red hat, sunglasses, a jacket, and an earpiece with a green wire. Those were our only clues. Now that the thief is not wearing this stuff we'll never find him."

"I'm giving this hat to the police. And I'm telling them where to find these other things," Mrs. Wayne said. "Then we have to get to the park."

Because of the fence, there was no way out

of the backyard except down the driveway.

"Look!" Mrs. Wayne said. "We don't have to walk around. There's a back door to the bakery."

Mrs. Wayne opened the door. She, Cam, and Eric walked past large ovens, two women mixing dough, a young man decorating a cake with icing, and a young man taking loaves of bread from an open oven.

"You can't be here," one of the women told Mrs. Wayne, Cam, and Eric.

"They're with me," Mrs. Wayne said. "I'm Dr. Prell's secretary. She's the principal."

"This is a bakery, not a school," one of the women told Mrs. Wayne.

"Okay," Mrs. Wayne said. "We're leaving."

She walked with Cam and Eric past the workers to the front of the store.

One of the police officers was a tall woman. The other was a not-so-tall man with a short beard.

"Hey, aren't you the clicking girl?" the not-so-tall officer with the short beard asked

Cam. "Do you remember me? I'm Officer Gil Oppen. I met you at your school."

"I'm Officer Davis," his partner told Cam.

"I remember both of you," Cam said.

Mrs. Wayne pointed to Cam's head and said, "She remembers everything. She's got a camera and photo albums in that head of hers."

Mrs. Wayne gave Officer Oppen the large red hat. Eric told the police officers about the sunglasses and jacket.

"They're in back, in the trash bin," Cam said. "We think the thief wore them."

Officer Oppen said to his partner, "We knew what the thief was wearing. Now he's not wearing any of it."

"Don't worry," Officer Davis told Zelda. "We'll still look for him."

"We have to go," Mrs. Wayne told the two police officers.

"Today is Sports Day. We're on our way to Franklin Park."

Mrs. Wayne, Cam, and Eric left Zelda's.

Danny, Beth, and Mr. Pace were waiting outside. Cam and Eric told them about the things they found in the trash bin. Then they hurried to catch up with their class.

Chapter Four

Mrs. Wayne and Mr. Pace led Cam, Eric, Beth, and Danny to the entrance to Franklin Park.

"There you are," Ms. Benson said. "We were waiting for you."

Trill! Trill!

Mr. Day, the gym teacher, blew a whistle.

"Follow me," he shouted.

"Stay together," Ms. Benson said. "Don't wander off."

Eric whispered to Cam, "Maybe she's afraid the thief is in the park."

Everyone in Ms. Benson's and Mr. Dane's classes followed Mr. Day through the park.

They walked on the path along the edge of the lake. They walked past a soccer field, a baseball field, and a picnic area. They walked past a playground with swings and a fenced-in sandbox.

"Here we are," Mr. Day shouted.

They had reached a fenced-in track with white lines painted on the ground.

"The egg-balancing race is first," Mr. Day said.

He put an egg on a spoon and walked with it.

"That's all you have to do. You have to walk to the finish line without dropping the egg. The first one there wins."

"Is that a raw egg?" someone asked.

"Let's see."

Mr. Day shook his spoon. The egg fell to the ground and broke.

"*Yuck!*" Beth and a few others said.

Danny waved and said, "Bye-bye, Mr. Egg. I guess you cracked up because my jokes are so funny."

"I need six from each class," Mr. Day said.

"I'll race," Danny said. "I'm good with eggs."

The twelve children stood at the starting line. Mr. Day gave them each a spoon and an egg.

"Hey," Danny asked the boy next to him. "Do you know what goes up white and comes down yellow?"

The boy held his spoon steady. When Danny asked his riddle, the boy didn't move. He didn't answer Danny.

"On your marks," Mr. Day said. "Get set. Go!"

Eleven of the children started to walk. They held their spoons out and took slow but steady steps.

"Go! Go! Go!" people called out.

"It's an egg," Danny called to the boy who had been next to him. "An egg goes up white and comes down yellow."

No one but Danny heard his joke. Everyone else was either holding an egg on a spoon and taking careful steady steps or watching the race.

"Go!" Mr. Pace called to his son. "Go!"

"Hey! Wait for me," Danny said.

Danny took a long quick step, and his egg fell.

"Look," Danny said. He pointed to the broken egg. "It was white up here and now it's yellow."

Eric was watching the race. Cam wasn't. Her eyes were closed. She was thinking about the robbery at Zelda's.

"Those two women, Sadie and Martha,

went out one way from Zelda's," Cam said with her eyes closed. "Four other people went out the other way. I have a picture in my head of them leaving Zelda's. One was wearing a red hat."

"Really?" Eric asked. "He's the thief."

"We only know what he *was* wearing," Cam said. "And now he's not wearing it."

People cheered.

Cam opened her eyes.

Jacob was the first to reach the finish line without breaking his egg. Fernando finished second. Sarah was third. They were all in Mr. Dane's class.

"The potato-sack race is next," Mr. Day said. "I need six from each class."

Eric said, "I'm racing this time."

"I'm racing, too," Beth said. "And I hope someone from our class wins."

Chapter Five

"Mr. Dane's class won the egg race," Beth said. "This time we'll win!"

Mr. Day gave Eric, Beth, and each of the others in the potato-sack race a large cloth bag.

"Climb in," he told them. "When you run, your feet and legs must be in the bag."

Eric stepped into the bag.

"On your marks," Mr. Day said. "Get set. Go!"

Eric took a big step forward and fell. Lots of runners fell. They got up, took another big step, and fell again.

Cam walked along the side of the track. She leaned over the fence and whispered to Eric, "Take small steps."

Eric got up. He held on to the top of his cloth bag. He took one small step and then another.

Beth took a big step and fell.

Eric didn't hurry. He took only small steps. He didn't fall. Soon he was ahead of everyone.

"Go! Go! Go!" Cam called.

Eric went. He took small steps and didn't fall again. He was the first to reach the finish line. Tamika and Shane from Mr. Dane's class came in second and third.

Beth took a giant step just before the finish line and fell. She looked up at Eric and said, "Good. I'm glad one of us won."

Eric stepped out of his cloth bag. He turned and began to walk back to the starting line.

"Don't go that way," Ms. Benson told him. "Walk around. We're setting up for the next race."

Eric walked past the finish line again. He walked around the fence along the side of the track.

"You were right," Eric told Cam. "I didn't take big steps and I didn't fall."

"Let's go! Let's go," Mr. Day called out. "The backward race is next. Anyone who wasn't in the first two races must be in the backward race."

"That's me," Cam said.

"Line up right here," Mr. Day said. "Stand backward."

Cam stood on the starting line. She was facing Mr. Day. Beyond him was the sandbox. A young child sitting in the sand had lost his shovel. He started to cry.

"It's right there," his mother told him. "It's right behind you." She was sitting on a bench beside the fenced-in sandbox.

The small boy didn't turn. He just cried louder.

"No turning around to run forward," Mr. Day told Cam and the others in the backward race. "You must run backward."

The small boy's mother stretched over the low fence that surrounded the sandbox. She couldn't reach the shovel. The small boy cried louder.

"I'll be right there," his mother said.

She ran around the fence. She reached behind her son and gave him the shovel.

"That's it!" Cam said.

Cam closed her eyes and said, *"Click!"*

"On your marks," Mr. Day called. "Get set. Go!"

Cam's eyes were still closed. She said, *"Click!"* again.

The others in the backward race ran backward.

"Run Cam! Run!" Beth, Danny, and Mr. Pace called.

"Open your eyes," Eric called to Cam. "Start running. Everyone is way ahead of you."

Eric shook his head.

"No," he said. "They're way behind you, and in the backward race that means they're way ahead of you. You're losing the race."

Cam opened her eyes. She turned and looked behind her. She started to run backward.

As Cam passed Eric she told him, "I know how to find the thief."

"Just run," Eric said.

Cam ran, but she was the last to cross the finish line. Mr. Dane's class had won again.

"Don't worry," Beth said. "We'll win the soccer and baseball games."

Cam hurried from the finish line to the starting line.

"I have to go back to Zelda's," Cam told Ms. Benson. "I may have solved the mystery. I might know how to catch the bakery thief."

Chapter Six

"Can you really catch the thief?" Eric asked.

"I think so," Cam said. "Please, Ms. Benson. Let me go to Zelda's."

Ms. Benson told Cam, "You can't go alone."

Eric said, "I'll go with her."

"No," Ms. Benson said. "You need to go with an adult."

"I'll go, too," Mrs. Wayne said. "I want to help Cam Jansen catch that man. I also love Zelda's." She closed her eyes and took a deep breath. "That whole place smells like bread, cookies, and cupcakes."

"Go ahead," Ms. Benson told Cam. "But hurry back. We're resting a short while and then we're playing soccer."

Cam, Eric, and Mrs. Wayne walked past the fenced-in sandbox, picnic area, baseball field, and soccer field.

Mrs. Wayne said, "I bet I could find Zelda's with my eyes closed. I just have to walk straight ahead, and when I smell bread, cookies, and cupcakes, I'll know I'm there."

Mrs. Wayne closed her eyes and walked ahead. She walked right into a tree.

"I'm sorry," Mrs. Wayne told the tree. Then she opened her eyes.

"Oh," she said. "You're a maple tree. I can tell what tree you are by your leaves."

"Do you remember what happened after the potato-sack race?" Cam asked.

"I won," Eric said.

"Yes. And you had to walk around the fence to come back to the starting line. That happened in the sandbox, too," Cam said. "The boy had to wait for his mother to walk around the fence."

Cam, Eric, and Mrs. Wayne were at the corner. They looked both ways. No cars were coming, so they crossed the street.

"Do you remember the driveway next to Zelda's?" Cam asked. "The bakery was on one side. The other side was fenced in. We saw the thief leave Zelda's. But then we were talking to Martha and Sadie. We didn't see where the thief went. Now we know he must have gone along the driveway and dropped his hat, sunglasses, jacket, and earphones in the trash bin."

"Of course, he must have gone there," Eric said. "That's where we found his things."

"That was his plan," Mrs. Wayne said. "He wanted us to remember his floppy hat and sunglasses. Then he threw it all away."

"Yes," Cam said as they walked. "But where did he go after that?"

Mrs. Wayne and Eric didn't know.

Cam said, "I watched Zelda's and I didn't see anyone walk out from the driveway. If he didn't leave by the driveway, he must have gone through the back door of the bakery."

"If he did," Eric said, "the workers saw him."

"Yes. And they saw him without his disguise. Maybe they can describe him."

"We're almost there," Mrs. Wayne said, and took a deep breath. "I can already smell the bread."

They stopped by the door to the bakery and looked in.

A woman was standing by the counter. She was buying a loaf of bread. Officers Oppen and Davis were still there. They were talking to Zelda.

"Officer Oppen," Cam said when she went in. "I have to talk to you."

"Is it about the robbery?"

Cam nodded.

Officer Oppen and Cam went to a quiet place near the front of the bakery. Cam told him everything she had told Eric and Mrs. Wayne.

"If the thief came in the back door," Cam

said, "the workers saw him without his floppy hat and sunglasses. They can tell you what he looks like."

"Come with me," Officer Oppen said. "We'll ask them."

Officer Oppen and Cam went behind the counter to the back of the bakery. Two women and two men were working. They were the same people Cam, Eric, and Mrs. Wayne had seen there earlier.

"I need to talk to you," Officer Oppen said.

The two women and one of the men stopped what they were doing. They went to where Officer Oppen and Cam were standing. The other man turned and started toward the back door of the bakery.

Cam looked at him. She closed her eyes and said, "*Click!*

"Stop him!" Cam said with her eyes still closed. "Don't let him get away!"

Chapter Seven

Officer Oppen hurried to the back door. "Don't go anywhere," he told the bakery worker. "We need to talk to you."

Cam opened her eyes.

"Sadie and Martha told us the thief was wearing blue jeans and blue sneakers," Cam said.

Officer Oppen looked at the worker's jeans and sneakers. They were blue.

"I didn't hurt anyone," the worker said. "I just took some money and a bracelet. I'll give it all back."

"It's the new boy," one of the bakery women said.

"Tom, are you the thief?" the other woman asked.

Tom didn't answer.

Officer Oppen took out a pair of hand-cuffs. He locked them around Tom's wrists.

"Come with me," Officer Oppen said.

Tom, Officer Oppen, and Cam went to the front of the bakery.

"We have our thief," Officer Oppen told Zelda.

"I'm really sorry," Tom said. "I shouldn't have robbed your customers. But I didn't

hurt them. All the money and the bracelet are in my pockets."

"May I empty them?" Officer Oppen asked.

Tom nodded.

He emptied Tom's pockets and gave Zelda the bracelet and all the money Tom had taken.

"You're done here!" Zelda said. "You're fired!"

She looked at the bracelet and money. "I know who he robbed," Zelda told the two police officers. "I'll return everything."

Officer Oppen said, "I didn't know how we'd find the thief. But this girl did."

Officer Davis asked Tom. "Did you really think you could get away with this?"

Tom nodded. "Early this morning," he said, "I hid the hat and other things behind the bakery. During my break I went out the back way and put them on. Then, when I came in through the front door, no one knew it was me."

"Cam Jansen knew," Eric said.

Officer Davis told Cam, "You would make a great detective."

"She's also a good student," Mrs. Wayne said. "I know. I'm the principal's secretary."

Officer Oppen told Zelda, "I think you should reward these children."

"Of course," Zelda said. "You can have all the cookies you want or my famous sprinkle cupcakes."

"Today is Sports and Good Nutrition Day," Mrs. Wayne said. "The school's principal will be telling everyone to eat good foods and get lots of exercise."

Mrs. Wayne looked down. Her voice got lower.

"I'm sorry to say this, but cookies and cupcakes have lots of sugar. It's not the best food for children to eat."

"My cookies and sprinkle cupcakes are delicious," Zelda said. "But if you want, I'll give you oat bran, whole wheat, and corn muffins. I use very little sugar in my muffins and I use applesauce instead of butter. They're delicious and they're good for you."

"Thank you," Mrs. Wayne said. "And can you give us forty-six? We really need enough for every child in the fifth grade."

"Forty-six muffins!" Zelda said. "That's a lot." Then she smiled and said, "Of course you can have them. The muffins are still warm. They just came out of the oven."

Officers Oppen and Davis thanked Cam. Then they led Tom out of the bakery.

Zelda filled four bags with warm muffins and gave them to Cam, Eric, and Mrs. Wayne.

Eric took the card Sadie had given him and gave it to Zelda.

"When you return her things," Eric said, "please tell her the red-haired girl with the great memory caught the thief. I told her Cam would get her things back. I want her to know I was right."

"Yes," Zelda said, and smiled. "I'll tell her."

Cam, Eric, and Mrs. Wayne left the bakery. Eric carried two of the muffin bags. Cam and Mrs. Wayne each had one.

As they walked, Mrs. Wayne opened her bag. She took a deep breath. "Ah," she said. "I love the smell of fresh muffins.

Eric said, "I love eating fresh muffins."

"I love muffins, too," Cam said. "And I love solving mysteries."

CamJansen

The Soccer Game Mystery

Chapter One

Mrs. Wayne looked in the bakery bag she was carrying. "I'll bet these muffins taste good," she said as she walked with Cam and Eric to Franklin Park.

Mrs. Wayne took an oat bran muffin from the bag.

"Yummy. This smells so good," she said as she held the muffin close to her nose. "Do you think I could have one?"

"You can have mine," Eric told her.

"No," Mrs. Wayne said. "I won't take yours."

They had come to the park entrance.

"Oops!" Mrs. Wayne said. "This muffin touched my nose. No one will want it now. I guess I should eat it."

"Sure," Cam said. "We'll have enough. Eric and I will share one."

"No," Mrs. Wayne told them. "Three children are absent today. Let's just say this is one of theirs."

Mrs. Wayne bit into the muffin. "Eghen flugh zgats joosd flogh joo sjan zgaste joosd," she said with her mouth full.

"What?" Cam asked Mrs. Wayne. "What did you say?"

Mrs. Wayne swallowed.

"I said, 'Even food that's good for you can taste good.'"

Mrs. Wayne finished her oat bran muffin. She walked with Cam and Eric along a path at the edge of the lake.

"Look at the boats," Mrs. Wayne said. "Mr. Wayne and I sometimes rent one. I like to row. It's good exercise."

The boat rental booth was right there, at the edge of the lake. There were several boats on the lake. Most were close to the booth.

"Look," Mrs. Wayne said. "There's boat number seven. That's the one we had the last time we were here."

Mrs. Wayne smiled. "That was such a nice day. Please," she said to Cam, "take a picture with your mental camera of boat number seven."

Cam looked at the boat. She blinked her eyes and said, *"Click!"*

The soccer field was on the other side of the path.

Zoom!

A toy car sped in front of Cam, Eric, and Mrs. Wayne.

"Yikes!" Mrs. Wayne said. "I almost stepped on a car."

An old man was sitting on a bench beside the path. He held a remote-control unit.

"Watch out!" the man said. Then he pushed a button and the car crossed the path again.

Zoom!

An old woman at the next bench put down her newspaper. "Sam," she said. "Be careful with that!"

The man pushed another button. The car turned and sped right in front of Mrs. Wayne, Cam, and Eric. It went right into the old woman's foot.

"Oh, I'm sorry," Sam said.

The woman took the toy car and gave it to Sam. "Please, be careful with this," she said very loudly.

"Sam is my husband," the woman told Mrs. Wayne, Cam, and Eric. "He doesn't hear or see very well."

Cam, Eric, and Mrs. Wayne walked onto the soccer field. Eric told his classmates, Ms. Benson, and Mr. Day about the bakery thief and how Cam had caught him. Mrs. Wayne told everyone about the oat bran, whole wheat, and corn muffins.

"Hey," Danny said. "I like jelly doughnuts."

Beth said, "I like the rainbow-sprinkle cupcakes."

"This is not a doughnut and cupcake day," Ms. Benson said. "It's more of a muffin day, and you'll eat them later."

"Yes," Mr. Day said. "Now it's time to play soccer. You'll all get to play. Some of you will play the first half of the game. The others will play the second half."

Trill! Trill!

Mr. Day blew his whistle. He waved to Ms. Benson's and Mr. Day's classes. They gathered around him.

Mr. Day looked at everyone.

"You're a good player," he told Beth. "You'll play goalie. Felix, you'll be the goalie for Mr. Dane's team."

Mr. Day chose the other children who would play the first half. Cam and Eric would play the second half.

Trill! Trill!

Mr. Day blew his whistle to start the game.

Chapter Two

Mr. Day put the soccer ball in the center of the field. He blew his whistle and a player from Mr. Dane's class kicked the ball hard. It bounced and then rolled toward the goal. Beth grabbed the ball and threw it the other way.

"Good play," Ms. Benson shouted.

Players from both teams ran to the ball. They crowded around it. Each player tried to kick the ball toward his team's goal.

"Pass the ball! Pass the ball," Mr. Dane shouted. "Move it down the field."

The ball was stuck in the middle of the crowd. Players from both teams kicked it, but it just bounced and rolled from one player to another.

"Ow!" Carlos shouted. "Someone kicked me."

Carlos stepped away from the others. He rubbed his leg.

Someone from Ms. Benson's class kicked the ball hard. It rolled through the other players' legs toward the goal. Players from both teams raced after the ball.

"Here I come," Danny called.

Danny swung his foot far back and then forward. He missed the ball and fell.

"Not so hard," Ms. Benson shouted.

"Pass the ball," Hector shouted to the players on Ms. Benson's team.

Sam's remote-controlled toy car rode onto the field.

"Sam, turn the car around!" his wife told him. "Turn it around!"

Sam didn't seem to hear her.

Amy ran to the ball and kicked it toward the goal.

Sam's wife ran onto the field.

Felix, the goalie on Mr. Dane's team, caught the ball. He threw it toward the center of the field. It bounced onto the roof of Sam's remote-controlled toy car.

Sam's wife grabbed the toy car.

"Sam, you must be more careful," she told her husband as she hurried off the field.

"What?"

"Be careful!" she shouted.

Trill!

Mr. Day stopped the game. When Sam

and his wife were off the field, he gave the
ball to Dwayne, a boy in Mr. Dane's class.
Dwayne stood by the sideline. He held the
soccer ball over his head and threw it onto
the field.

"Here I come," Danny yelled again.

Danny ran to the ball. He quickly swung
his foot far back and kicked the ball hard. It
flew high into the air. It flew off to the side
and way beyond the field.

"Wow," Danny said.

The ball had gone high over Mr. Day's

head. It flew beyond the benches along the path.

"I'll get it," Eric shouted.

Eric ran off the field. He looked around. "Hey," he said. "Where did it go?"

Players from both teams joined Eric. They helped him look for the ball.

Between the path and the lake were lots of bushes. The players searched in the bushes.

"It's not here," Eric said. "It's not anywhere."

"It must be somewhere," Cam said. "Soccer balls don't just disappear."

"Well this one did," Danny said. "I kicked it way into outer space."

Chapter Three

Trill!

Mr. Day blew his whistle. He left the field and walked onto the path. "What's taking you so long?" he asked. "We're in the middle of a game."

"We can't find the ball," Eric answered.

"This time I really kicked it far," Danny said. "I didn't know I was so good at soccer."

"Well, those of you who are not playing can keep looking for the ball," Mr. Day said. "But those in the game should get back on the field. We'll use one of the practice balls."

Cam and Eric watched the players return to the field.

"My son lost the ball," Mr. Pace said, "so I'll help you find it."

"I'll also help," Hector said.

"We looked in the bushes and on the path. Where else could it be?" Eric asked.

"Maybe it's in the lake," Hector said.

"A soccer ball is filled with air," Cam said. "It would float."

Cam, Eric, Hector, and Mr. Pace walked to the edge of the lake. They saw a few boats in the water, a few ducks, and some branches. They didn't see the ball.

"Where could it be?" Eric asked.

"It's probably in the bushes," Mr. Pace said. "Lots of people looked there, but they weren't organized. Maybe they all looked in the same few bushes. Maybe they missed the one with the ball. We should look again."

"We'll start at one end of the row of bushes," Eric said. "We'll keep looking until we find the ball."

The bushes were high and thick. Cam,

Eric, Hector, and Mr. Pace started at the bushes at the beginning of the path. They spread apart the branches of one bush after another. They found candy wrappers and a Frisbee. They didn't find the soccer ball.

"That's it," Hector said when they came to the last bush. "We checked them all."

"Maybe it landed on the path and rolled away," Mr. Pace said. "It could have rolled all the way to the other end of the park."

"It wouldn't roll away," Hector said. "Both ways from here the path goes uphill."

"Maybe someone walking by caught it," Eric said. "Maybe he took it home."

"I don't think so," Cam said. "We got here right after Danny kicked the ball. If someone caught it, we would have seen him."

"Things don't just disappear," Mr. Pace said. "I know. I once did magic on stage."

"You did?" Eric asked.

"Yes, and Mrs. Pace was my assistant. My best trick was dropping a cloth over her and saying a few magic words. I lifted the cloth and she was gone."

"Wow!" Hector said.

"She didn't really disappear," Mr. Pace said. "There was a trapdoor under her chair. She snuck through it to the basement. She waited for me in the car."

"That's good," Hector said.

"Sure it's good," Mr. Pace said. "I would miss her if she really disappeared."

Eric turned. First he looked at the soccer field. He turned slowly and looked up the path toward the baseball field, at the lake, and then toward the park entrance. "This is some mystery," Eric said.

When Eric said the word "mystery," he looked at Cam. Hector and Mr. Pace also looked at her.

"What?" Cam asked.

Mr. Pace asked her, "Don't you solve mysteries?"

"Sometimes," Cam answered.

"Well, please try to solve this one."

Chapter Four

Trill! Trill!

Mr. Day blew his whistle.

"Let's go!" he called to Cam, Eric, and Hector. "It's your turn to play."

Cam, Eric, and Hector crossed the path and walked onto the field. "Let's see if you can kick the ball as far as I did," Danny said as he walked to the sidelines. "I kicked a home run!"

"I wish you had kicked it into the goal," Hector told him. "Then we would be ahead."

"What's the score?" Eric asked Beth.

"It's tied, one to one."

Mr. Day told Eric, "It's your turn to be goalie for Ms. Benson's team. Sarah, you'll be the goalie for Mr. Dane's team."

Eric and Sarah each walked to a different end of the field. They stood in front of their goals.

Hector stood in the center of the field. Mr. Day blew his whistle. He dropped the ball and Hector kicked it toward Sarah. A player from Mr. Dane's team stopped the ball with his foot. He kicked the ball the other way.

"Pass the ball! Pass the ball!" Mr. Dane shouted. "Move it down the field."

Players from both teams ran toward Eric's goal. Mr. Day ran with them.

A player from Mr. Dane's team kicked the ball to another player on his team. They kicked it from one to another as they hurried toward Eric.

Eric stood by the goal and waited.

Fernando, a boy in Mr. Dane's class, kicked the ball hard. It flew fast and straight toward the goal.

Eric jumped. He caught the ball before it reached the goal. He threw it toward Cam.

"Good play," Ms. Benson yelled to Eric.

Cam didn't see the ball coming. She was thinking about the missing soccer ball.

"Pay attention," Hector said as he ran in front of Cam.

Hector kicked the ball toward Sarah and the other goal.

Players from both teams ran toward Sarah's goal. Mr. Day ran with them.

Then Hector kicked the ball hard. It flew past Sarah and into the net.

Trill! Mr. Day blew his whistle. "That's a goal," he shouted.

Mr. Day stopped running. He took a deep breath. "Let's rest a minute," he said.

Cam stopped. She looked toward the path and thought about the missing soccer ball. She saw Sam. He was still playing with the remote-controlled toy car.

"Sam," his wife called as she put down her newspaper. "Sam!" she shouted.

Sam turned and his wife pointed to the toy car. Sam pushed a button on his remote control. The car turned and went right to her.

Sam's wife opened her purse. She took out a pen and a small sheet of paper. She wrote a note and stuck it onto the car's antenna. Sam pushed a button and the car traveled back to him.

Sam's wife opened a bag that was on her bench. She took out two wrapped sandwiches and two juice containers.

Sam took the note off the car and read it.

"Good," he said, and laughed. "I'm hungry."

Sam picked up his car. He joined his wife on the next bench. They unwrapped the sandwiches and began to eat lunch.

Trill!

"Let's go!" Mr. Day shouted. "Let's finish the game."

Mr. Day placed the ball in the center of the field. A player from Mr. Dane's team kicked it toward Eric's goal.

Cam stood by the sideline. She watched Sam and his wife eating. The toy car was on the bench.

"That's it!" Cam said. "That's where I'll find the soccer ball."

Chapter Five

Cam ran off the soccer field.

"Hey," Ms. Benson yelled. "Where are you going?"

Trill! Trill! Mr. Day blew his whistle.

"Get back here!" he shouted.

"I think I know where to find the missing soccer ball," Cam said as she ran off the field. Mr. Day followed her.

Cam ran across the path to the edge of the lake. She waved her hands. "Look in your boat. Is there a soccer ball in your boat?"

A man and a woman in a boat near the edge of the lake looked at Cam. Then they looked in their boat and shook their heads. They didn't find the ball. The others in boats didn't look at Cam. They hadn't heard her.

Eric ran to Cam.

"What are you doing?" he asked. "We're in the middle of a game."

Ms. Benson, Hector, Sarah, and others also hurried toward Cam.

"I know what happened to the soccer ball," Cam said. "I know why we didn't find it."

"Hey," Mr. Day said as he walked toward Cam. "You can't just run off the field."

"Did you see when Sam's wife stuck the note onto the antenna of his car? The car carried the note to Sam. Well, I think that's what happed with our soccer ball. I think it landed in one of the boats when it was close to the path. Then the boat carried it away."

"That could have happened," Hector said. "But wouldn't someone know if a ball landed in his boat?"

"Maybe it landed behind him," Eric said. "Maybe he's like Sam, the man with the remote-controlled car. Maybe he doesn't hear very well."

"You have a loud voice," Cam said to Mr. Day. "Can you call to the people in the boats and ask them if they have our soccer ball?"

"Hey!" Mr. Day shouted. "Is there a soccer ball in your boat?"

People in boats 7 and 4 turned toward Mr. Day. They shook their heads.

The old man in boat 6 kept rowing.

Trill! Trill! Mr. Day blew his whistle. He waved to the man. But the man didn't turn.

"He's rowing toward shore," Ms. Benson said. "I'll wait for him."

"We can't wait for him to get back here," Mr. Day said. "We've got a game to play."

Mr. Day went to the rental booth. Cam, Eric, Ms. Benson, and others followed him.

"How do you call to the boaters?"

The woman in the booth showed Mr. Day a megaphone. She let him borrow it.

Mr. Day stood at the edge of the lake. He blew his whistle into the megaphone.

Trill! Trill!

Cam, Eric, and many others along the lake held their hands to their ears. People in the boats turned. Even the man in boat 6 turned.

Mr. Day pointed to the man in boat 6. Then he shouted to him through the megaphone, "Please, look behind you. Is there a soccer ball in your boat?"

The man looked in front of him. Then he shook his head. He didn't find the soccer ball.

"Please," Mr. Day shouted through the megaphone. "Turn and look behind you."

The man turned. He turned again and faced Mr. Day. This time he nodded. Then he reached back and held up a soccer ball.

"Yeah!" Eric said. "Cam solved another mystery."

"Thank you," Mr. Day and Ms. Benson said to Cam.

"I'll wait here," Ms. Benson said. "I'll get the ball when he brings in the boat."

"Let's go," Mr. Day said. "Let's finish the game."

Ms. Benson waited by the edge of the lake. Everyone else returned to the soccer field. Now that she had solved the mystery, Cam was able to pay attention to the game. She even kicked the ball, but she didn't score a goal. Still, Ms. Benson's team won the game 2–1.

Cam Jansen

The Baseball Glove Mystery

Chapter One

"What did you bring for lunch?" Eric asked Cam.

Cam unwrapped her sandwich.

"Cream cheese."

"Yuck!" Danny said. "That's so dry."

"Well, I like it," Cam told him.

"It has lots of calcium," Mr. Pace said. "It's good for Cam's bones."

Cam, Eric, Danny, and Danny's father were sitting at a picnic table in Franklin Park. Beth, Hector, and others from Ms. Benson's class were sitting with them. After lunch, their principal, Dr. Prell, would speak to the fifth graders about eating good food and getting lots of exercise. Then they would play baseball.

"Hey, cream cheese is dry and here's a dry joke," Danny said. "I say 'Knock knock' and you say 'Who's there?' Okay?"

Eric nodded.

"Knock knock," Danny started.

"Who's there?" Eric asked.

"Orange," Danny answered.

"Orange who?" Hector asked.

"Orange you glad I'm telling jokes?" Danny answered.

"I'm only glad," Beth told him, "if the jokes are funny."

"Okay, Beth. Here's a funny orange joke. Why did the orange lose the race?"

Beth shook her head. She didn't know.

"It ran out of juice," Danny said. "That's why it lost."

Beth smiled.

"Okay," she said. "That was funny."

"All this juice talk has made me thirsty," Cam said.

Hector told Cam, "Ms. Benson said she

has drinks for us. She's at the table with Mr. Dane, Mr. Day, Dr. Prell, and Mrs. Wayne."

"It won't be soda. That's for sure," Danny said. "I'll bet it's some drink with vitamins and healthy stuff."

"My dad calls soda 'sugar water with bubbles,'" Hector said. "He won't let me drink it."

Cam and Eric went to Ms. Benson's table.

"What would you like to drink?" Ms. Benson asked. "You can have orange juice, milk, or water."

Cam chose water. Eric took orange juice.

Dr. Prell told Cam to take something from a large tray of sliced fruits and vegetables. Cam took a carrot stick. Eric took apple and orange slices.

Mrs. Wayne held an open bakery bag in front of Cam. "Take a muffin. Cam Jansen caught a thief at Zelda's Bakery and Zelda gave us lots of muffins·as a reward."

Cam reached into the bag. She took an oat bran muffin.

"Oh, my," Mrs. Wayne said. "It's you. You're Cam Jansen! You're the *clicking* girl!"

"*Click!*" Cam said, and smiled.

Eric took a corn muffin.

"Muffins are no fun," Danny said when Cam and Eric returned to their table. "But memory quizzes are. Cam, click and close your eyes. I'll quiz you."

Cam looked at the people at her table. She blinked her eyes and said, "*Click!*" She looked at the people at the other tables, and on the benches. She looked at the signs by the tables, too. Cam closed her eyes and said, "*Click!*"

"Yesterday," Danny asked, "what did I wear to school?"

"Hey, that's not fair," Eric said.

Cam laughed. "I remember. You wore a T-shirt that said, 'My Sister Did It!'"

"That's real funny," Danny said, "because I don't have a sister."

No one laughed.

"Okay," Danny said. "What color is Beth's shirt?"

"Green," Cam told him. "Her shorts are blue and her sneakers are white."

"Yes," Beth said. "These sneakers are new."

"Hmm," Danny said. He looked around and asked, "There's a teenager at one of the benches eating a large candy bar. What color is his shirt?"

"Purple," Cam said with her eyes still closed. "He's also wearing beads and yellow pants."

"That's right," Danny said. "There's a girl sitting with him. What about her hair?"

"It's black, green, and purple," Cam answered.

"That's right," Eric said. "Cam is always right."

Trill! Trill!

Mr. Day blew his whistle. He held up his hands, and the fifth graders stopped talking. Cam opened her eyes.

Dr. Prell stood next to Mr. Day. She took a sheet of paper from her pocket. She was about to start her talk.

Chapter Two

Dr. Prell smiled. "I'm so happy to see all of you here," she said. "Getting exercise is important, and playing sports is a fun way to do it. It's also important to eat the right food. You should eat plenty of protein, whole grains, fruits, and vegetables."

Danny put on his baseball glove.

"You should drink plenty of milk, juice, and water," Dr. Prell said.

Danny punched the pocket of his glove and whispered, "We know all this stuff."

"Sh," his father whispered. "Listen to the principal."

"Soon you'll play a game of baseball," Dr.

Prell said. "One team will win. The other team will come in second. Neither team will lose, because by playing you'll be exercising, and that's good for you. And there will be a surprise for you when you're done." Dr. Prell held up two envelopes. "After the game each of you will get a special treat."

The principal gave one envelope to Ms. Benson and the other to Mr. Dane. "This will pay for the treats," she told the two teachers.

Children cheered.

Ms. Benson put the envelope in her purse. Mr. Dane tried to put his in his pocket, but it was too big.

"Can you hold mine?" he asked Ms. Benson.

Ms. Benson put Mr. Dane's envelope in her purse.

"Did you see those envelopes?" Hector whispered. "They're stuffed."

"They're filled with money," Eric said. "There are lots of kids, so that's lots of treats and lots of money."

"Have fun!" Dr. Prell said.

"We'll have fun," Danny said, and punched his glove again. "And we'll win!"

"Muffins!" Mrs. Wayne called out as she went from table to table. She held out a bakery bag and asked, "Who wants muffins?"

Danny reached into the bag. He took out a muffin.

"Hey," Danny said. "What flavor is this?"

Beth laughed. "It's just like you," she said. "It's corny."

Trill!

Mr. Day blew his whistle. He held up his hands and everyone was quiet.

"Eat slowly," he said. "And when you're finished, sit by your tables and rest. At one o'clock we'll play baseball."

"Did you bring a glove?" Danny asked Cam and Eric.

Cam shook her head. "We're not all playing the field at the same time. I'll borrow one from someone. "

"Me, too," Eric said.

Danny punched the pocket of his glove. "You won't get a glove like this," he said. "It's my vacuum cleaner. It sweeps the field and catches everything."

Cam and the others finished eating. Danny told jokes while they rested and waited to play baseball. Then Mr. Day blew his whistle. It was time to start the game.

Chapter Three

Everyone went to the baseball field.

"Part of each class will play the first few innings," Mr. Day said. "The others will play after that. Ms. Benson's class is on the field first."

Danny punched his glove and said, "I'll play shortstop. My vacuum cleaner will get everything."

Ms. Benson told Eric to play third base. She told Cam, Beth, and Hector to play the outfield.

Trill!

"Play ball!" Mr. Day called out.

Amy was the first batter. She hit the ball on the ground and right at Danny.

Danny stood with his glove down and legs apart and waited for the ball. He watched the ball as it bounced quickly toward him. Then he turned and watched the ball as it bounced behind him.

Amy ran past first base. She stopped at second base with a double.

The next two batters hit the ball to the outfield. Beth caught the first ball. Hector caught the second.

Eric turned from his position at third base. "One more out," he called to the team. "Then it's our turn to bat."

The next batter on Mr. Dane's team hit the ball to shortstop. Danny held up his glove and the ball flew right past him. Amy ran around third base and scored. Mr. Dane's team was ahead 1–0.

The next batter hit the ball on the ground toward third base. Eric reached to his right. He caught it and threw to first base in time to get the third out.

"Hey, what happened to you?" Hector asked Danny as Ms. Benson's class walked off the field. "I thought that glove was a vacuum cleaner."

There was a high metal fence behind home plate. Ms. Benson's team walked behind the fence. Most of the players dropped their gloves on the ground and sat on a long bench.

Danny still had his glove. He turned it over and looked at the back of it.

"Hey," Danny told Hector. "Here's the problem. It's the on-off switch. I forgot to turn my glove vacuum on."

"No," Hector said. "You forgot to catch the ball."

Sarah was the pitcher for Mr. Dane's team. Cam was the first of her team to bat. She hit the first pitch, a slow roller to third base. Cam ran quickly and was safe at first. Beth and Danny struck out. Eric hit the ball deep to centerfield, but the ball was caught for the third out. The inning was over.

After that first inning, there were a few hits but no more runs. Then, in the third inning, when there were two outs, Cam hit a single. Then Beth and Danny each hit a single. The bases were loaded. It was Eric's turn at bat.

"Get a hit!" Ms. Benson called out.

Many of Eric's classmates gathered behind the fence.

Eric stood at home plate. He took a few practice swings. Then he held his bat back and waited.

Sarah pitched the ball. It was high, way out of Eric's reach. He didn't swing.

"Ball one," Mr. Day called.

"Wait for a good one," Ms. Benson called out.

Cam stood at third base and watched. She was ready to run home. Beth stood on second base. Danny stood on first base. They were ready to run, too.

Sarah pitched the ball. This time it came in right over home plate.

Eric swung. He hit the ball high over the third baseman's head.

Everyone still sitting on the bench ran to the fence right behind home plate. Those in Ms. Benson's class hoped the ball would go over the left fielder's head. Mr. Dane's class hoped the ball would be caught.

Cam ran home. She crossed home plate. Then she turned to see what would happen. Beth and Danny were running toward home, too.

Felix, the left fielder, held up his glove.

The ball was over his head. He chased after it.

"Go! Go!" Ms. Benson called out.

Eric touched first base. He ran toward second. Felix chased after the ball.

"Go! Go!" Ms. Benson called again.

Eric ran from second to third. Felix grabbed the ball.

Eric touched third base and ran toward home. Felix threw the ball to Sarah who was standing in front of home plate. The ball reached Sarah before Eric did. Sarah tagged Eric.

"You're out, Eric!" Mr. Day shouted.

"That's okay," Danny said. "Three runs scored. We're winning, 3–1."

The players on Mr. Dane's team walked off the field. The players on Ms. Benson's team turned from the fence. They went back to the bench.

"Hey," Hector said. "Where's my glove?"

"Where's mine?" Danny asked.

"All our gloves are gone," Eric said. "Someone stole them."

Chapter Four

Beth said, "Maybe the gloves fell under the bench."

"All of them?" Hector asked.

Beth and Danny looked under the bench. The gloves weren't there.

"I think I saw someone run toward the lake," Ms. Benson said. "She ran off while Eric was running around the bases."

Ms. Benson hurried to the path toward the lake. Cam, Eric, and others in Ms. Benson's class followed her.

"Let's help," Mr. Dane told his class.

They ran to the path, too.

"Look," Eric said and pointed. "There she is."

"It's the girl who was sitting near us when we were eating lunch," Danny said. "It's the teenager with the black, green, and purple hair."

It was a winding path. It was also not a level path. The girl was at a high point. She had stopped running. She turned and was facing Ms. Benson and the others running toward her.

"Look," Hector said. "She has our gloves."

The girl stood there at the top of the hill and watched as everyone ran toward her.

"Why did she stop running?" Beth asked. "Doesn't she want to get away?"

"Let's just get her," Danny said. "I want my glove."

Ms. Benson, Mr. Dane, and their students ran up the hill. Then, just as they were getting close to the teenager, she turned and started to run again. When she turned she dropped one of the gloves.

"I hope that's mine," Danny said.

It wasn't. It was Beth's glove.

The girl ran down the hill toward the entrance to the park. She dropped gloves as she ran.

Eric said, "She can't hold them all."

"This is mine," Hector said, and picked up a glove.

"Here's mine," Danny said. He picked up his glove and hugged it.

The girl fell near the entrance to the park. She had just one glove. She threw it toward Ms. Benson and laughed.

"That was fun," she said. "That was great fun."

"This was *not* fun!" Ms. Benson told the girl. "Taking what doesn't belong to you is wrong. It's wrong even if you return what you stole."

"Wow!" the girl said, and laughed. "You are one serious lady."

"She's a teacher," Hector told her. "She's a good teacher."

Ms. Benson glared at the teenage girl for a moment.

The girl glared back at Ms. Benson.

Ms. Benson turned to her class. "Let's go back," she said. "Let's finish the game."

Ms. Benson and Mr. Dane started to slowly walk back. Cam, Eric, and the others followed her.

Eric told Cam, "That was a strange joke."

Cam turned. She looked back to the park entrance. The girl was no longer on the ground. She was on her way out of Franklin Park.

"This whole thing is strange," Cam said. "And I don't think it was a joke."

Cam, Eric, and the others followed Ms. Benson back toward the baseball field.

"Oh, my!" Cam Jansen said.

Cam looked at Ms. Benson, closed her eyes, and said, *"Click!"*

"Quick!" Cam told Eric when she opened her eyes. "We have to find Danny's father. He said he has a cell phone. He has to call the police."

Chapter Five

"Why do we have to call the police? And why do we have to find Mr. Pace?" Eric asked. "What about Ms. Benson? She's right here, and I'm sure she has a phone."

"Look at her," Cam said as she looked for Mr. Pace. "She doesn't have her purse with her cell phone. She must have left it by the baseball field when she ran to get our gloves."

Eric turned and looked at Ms. Benson. Cam was right. Ms. Benson didn't have her purse.

Cam and Eric ran ahead to find Mr. Pace. "Mr. Pace," Cam said when they caught up to him. "Please, dial 911. We need the police."

"Why?" he asked. "We have the gloves."

"Yes, why?" Eric asked.

"I think something else was stolen," Cam said. "I think that girl took the gloves to get us away from the baseball field. I think when we ran after the gloves, her friend took Ms. Benson's purse."

"Hey," Eric said. "The envelopes are in her purse, the ones with the money for our treats."

"That girl and her friend were right there when Dr. Prell gave Ms. Benson and Mr. Dane the money," Cam said. "I bet that's when they decided to take it."

"I don't know," Mr. Pace said. "Maybe taking the gloves was really just a joke. Maybe Ms. Benson's purse is still on the bench."

"I don't think so," Cam said. "While we were chasing the girl with the purple hair, where was her friend with the yellow pants?"

"Maybe he's on the lake," Mr. Pace said. "Maybe he rented a boat."

Cam shook her head and said, "I think she took our gloves just to get us away from the field. I think while we chased her, he grabbed Ms. Benson's purse and the envelopes from Dr. Prell."

"Let's go," Cam told Eric. "Let's find Ms. Benson."

Cam ran along the path. Eric and Mr. Pace followed her.

"Ms. Benson! Ms. Benson!" Cam called.

Cam's teacher stopped and turned.

"I think someone stole your purse," Cam said. "I think he stole Dr. Prell's envelopes."

"Oh, my!" Ms. Benson said. "I left my purse by the baseball field."

Eric and Mr. Pace caught up with Cam. Mr. Pace was breathing hard.

"I can't run so fast," Mr. Pace said.

Cam told Ms. Benson, "We'll go ahead. If your purse is not there, we'll call the police."

"I'll go with you," Ms. Benson said.

"Here's my phone," Mr. Pace said. "I can't keep up with you."

Mr. Pace gave his cell phone to Ms. Benson.

Cam, Eric, and Ms. Benson hurried toward the baseball field.

"There's the bench," Eric said and pointed when they were close to the field. "And there's something on it."

Cam, Eric, and Ms. Benson got closer to the bench. In the middle of it was Ms. Benson's purse.

"This time you were wrong," Eric said. "The purse wasn't stolen."

The purse was open. Ms. Benson looked inside of it.

"Cam wasn't wrong," Ms. Benson said. "The purse is here. But the envelopes are gone."

Chapter Six

Ms. Benson said, "I'm calling the police."

She pressed a few buttons on Mr. Pace's cell phone and held the phone to her ear.

"There has been a robbery at Franklin Park. Someone stole two envelopes filled with money. I have someone here who I think can describe the thief."

Ms. Benson gave the cell phone to Cam.

"This is Jennifer Jansen," Cam said. "Officer Oppen knows me. Just tell him it's the clicking girl."

Cam waited. Then she said, "Hello, Officer Oppen. I can describe the man who I think took the envelopes."

Cam closed her eyes and said, *"Click!"*

"He was wearing beads, a purple shirt, and yellow pants," Cam said with her eyes closed. "His friend ran out of Franklin Park toward Zelda's. Maybe you'll find them somewhere near the bakery."

Cam opened her eyes.

"Thank you," Cam told Officer Oppen. "We'll be at the baseball field."

Mr. Pace, Mr. Dane, and lots of Cam's schoolmates were on the baseball field.

Trill! Trill!

Mr. Day blew his whistle.

"Let's play ball!" he shouted. "Bring in the second teams. Anyone who wasn't playing during the first half of the game should play now."

Eric told Cam, "We're no longer playing."

"That's good," Cam said. "I keep thinking about the envelopes. If the ball came to me now, I would probably miss it."

Cam and Eric sat on the bench. Jared was pitching for Ms. Benson's team.

Jared threw the ball toward home plate. Shane swung and missed. Jared pitched again and Shane swung and missed.

"Look how slow he's throwing," Danny said.

"He's great," Sarah said. "Shane just can't wait to swing at those slow pitches. He's swinging too soon."

Jared's third pitch was even slower than the others. Shane swung again and missed.

"Strike three! You're out," Mr. Day said.

Sometimes Jared threw the ball very slowly. Other times he pitched fast. Mr. Dane's team swung at lots of his pitches, but they didn't hit any. The next two batters struck out.

"That's three outs," Mr. Day said.

"Pow!" Danny said as Ms. Benson's team walked off the field. "I'd hit one of Jared's pitches a thousand feet. Jared would throw the ball. I'd tell a few jokes, eat a jelly dough-nut, and then when the ball finally came over the plate, I'd hit it. Pow!"

Fernando was now pitching for Mr. Dane's team. He threw the ball very fast. The players on Ms. Benson's team had trouble hitting his pitches.

There were just a few hits over the next two innings, and no runs scored.

"Look!" Beth said.

She pointed to the narrow road that ran through the park. A police car was coming slowly toward them. It stopped by the baseball field. The driver's door opened and a police officer got out.

Eric said, "It's Officer Oppen."

He held up two envelopes and walked toward Ms. Benson and Mr. Dane.

"We caught the two who stole these," he said. He gave the envelopes to Ms. Benson. "They were a few blocks from the park, and they were running. Now they're both in the car. With the beads, purple shirt, and purple hair, it was easy to find them. Officer Davis and I will be taking them to the station house."

"Funny," Cam said. "The bakery thief wore odd clothes and a big red floppy hat so he wouldn't get caught. The two in your car wore odd clothes and that's *why* they were caught."

Officer Oppen said, "There's something else that's funny. Open the envelopes."

Ms. Benson opened one of the envelopes. She took out a pack of papers and looked at them. "These are coupons," she said. "Each one is for a piece of fruit at the Franklin Park Snack Bar."

"No money?" Cam asked.

Ms. Benson shook her head.

"No money for cake or cookies or ice cream?" Danny asked.

Ms. Benson shook her head again.

Officer Oppen said, "The two we caught with these envelopes were really surprised when we showed them what they stole. They wanted money, not fruit."

Tamika said, "I want fruit."

"So do I," Sarah said.

"Thanks to Cam," Ms. Benson said, "you can all have snacks."

Trill! Trill!

Mr. Day blew his whistle.

"The game is over," he announced. "Ms. Benson's class wins three to one."

"We won because of Eric," Danny said.

Ms. Benson and Mr. Dane gave out the coupons.

"You helped us catch the bakery thief and the coupon thieves," Officer Oppen told Cam. "You solved two mysteries today."

"No," Eric said. "She solved three mysteries today. She also found a missing soccer ball."

Officer Oppen laughed. "The day's not over," he said. "There's still time for Cam to solve lots more mysteries!"

"There's also time for lots more pictures," Cam said.

Cam blinked her eyes. She said, *"Click!"* and took a picture of laughing Officer Oppen.

Cam Jansen Memory Games

:::

Do you have a photographic memory?

Study the picture on the next page. Blink your eyes and say, *"Click!"* Then turn the page. See how many questions you can answer. Don't turn back to check your answers until you have answered all the questions.

Repeat for all the pictures that follow.

:::

1. How many people are in the picture?
2. Is anyone wearing long pants?
3. What's written on the banner?
4. What is Cam carrying?
5. What is Eric carrying?
6. In which hand is Beth holding the banner, her left or her right?

1. How many people are wearing chef's hats?
2. How many layers are there on the big layer cake?
3. Mrs. Wayne is the woman standing at the door with Cam and Eric. Is Mrs. Wayne wearing a dress?
4. Is anyone wearing a checkered scarf?
5. How many bakery workers are in the picture?

1. How many people are sitting on the bench?
2. Is the man wearing eyeglasses?
3. Where is his toy car?
4. What are the man and woman holding?
5. Is Eric in the picture?
6. Is the woman wearing a dress?

1. In the picture, how many people are chasing the girl?
2. What is the girl carrying?
3. Does the girl have both her feet on the ground?
4. What are the man and woman holding?
5. Is the girl wearing socks?
6. Is the girl wearing polka-dotted shorts?